WEDN

I AM WEDNESDAY

illustrated by Vivien Wu

 A GOLDEN BOOK • NEW YORK

All rights reserved. Published in the United States by Golden Books, an imprint of Random House Children's Books, a division of Penguin Random House LLC, 1745 Broadway, New York, NY 10019, and in Canada by Penguin Random House Canada Limited, Toronto. Golden Books, A Golden Book, A Little Golden Book, the G colophon, and the distinctive gold spine are registered trademarks of Penguin Random House LLC.

MGM™

rhcbooks.com

ISBN 978-0-593-89669-3 (trade) — ISBN 978-0-593-89670-9 (ebook)

Printed in the United States of America

10 9 8 7 6 5 4 3 2 1

Hello, Dear Reader.
I assume you are reading
this book because you're a
little like me. My name is
Wednesday Addams.

I'm not like other kids.

(And anyone who messes with my little brother finds that out the hard way.)

My father calls me his little storm
cloud, which is fitting because . . .

. . . my mother adores dark rainy days and thunderstorms. And my father adores my mother.

It's gross.

I was born on Friday the thirteenth, supposedly a day of very bad luck. My mother named me Wednesday after a line in a famous poem:

Wednesday's child is full of woe.

I am now being sent to Nevermore Academy.

Nevermore is a school for werewolves, vampires, gorgons, sirens, and other kinds of outcasts.

Whether or not I fit in as an outcast,
I know what I *do* like and what I *don't*
like. And *that* makes some people
uneasy, for some reason.

For example, I like **Thing**. My parents sent him to keep an eye on me at school, but I made him swear loyalty to me instead. Now my five-fingered friend gives me a hand with whatever I get up to . . .

. . . whether it's
playing music . . .

. . . or solving mysteries. And there are *a lot* of mysteries to solve at Nevermore.

My roommate, **Enid**,
is different from me.
She likes lots of color . . .
and unicorns.

Black is my color
and will do just fine for
almost every situation.

Enid is also a werewolf and a hugger. I like werewolves well enough . . .

. . . but hugs not so much.

(*You can let go now.*)

I like fencing, the
art of sword fighting.
It's a dangerous way to
get good exercise.

Today, **Bianca** is my opponent. She'll
do anything to win, so I like to best her
whenever I can. But I have to admit,
she's quite good with a sword.

Seeing as how we are about to
part, Dear Reader, I will admit to
liking one last thing—**dancing** . . .
when the music is to my liking.

People say my moves are strange, and that might be true—but I'm Wednesday Addams, and I believe . . .

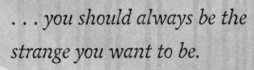

. . . you should always be the
strange you want to be.

No love. No kisses.
And definitely no hugs,
Wednesday Addams